MARGRET & H. A. REY'S

# Get Well, Curious George

Written by Julie M. Fenner

Illustrated in the style of H. A. Rey by Mary O'Keefe Young

Houghton Mifflin Harcourt

Boston   New York

George was a good little monkey and always very curious.
But one morning, George wasn't feeling quite as curious.
"What's wrong, George?" asked the man with the yellow hat.
George sneezed and pointed to his throat. "Does your throat
hurt?" asked his friend. George nodded his head yes.

The man put his hand on George's forehead. "You do feel a little warm. It looks like you may have caught a cold." George was confused. How do you "catch" a cold? He didn't remember playing catch yesterday.

"I'll call Dr. Sinha's office and make an appointment. In the meantime, you should lie down and rest."

The man found a thick, cozy blanket and fluffy pillows. George happily climbed onto the couch.

He brought George a glass of orange juice, crayons, and a coloring book and put George's favorite cartoon on the television.

George sipped his juice. It felt good on his sore throat.

He colored a few pictures.

He watched a cartoon.

Soon his eyelids started to feel heavy. The warmth of the blanket and pillows and the sounds from the television slowly lulled George to sleep.

Before he knew it, it was time to get up. "George, we need to leave for your doctor's appointment," said his friend as he gently rocked George awake.

George and his friend arrived
at Dr. Sinha's office.

"Be a good little monkey and don't wander off," said the
man, letting George down onto a waiting room chair. "I'll check
you in at the front desk."

George was too tired to wander off. He waited for the man to come back.

He was nervous to see the doctor.

"Don't worry, George. Everything will be okay," said the man as he sat down.

A nurse opened a nearby door and peered down at his clipboard. "George," he called. The man with the yellow hat took George's hand and they walked together to the exam room.

"Hi, George," said Dr. Sinha. "I hear you're not feeling well." George nodded his head. "Well, let's take a look."

Dr. Sinha examined George's sore throat and took his temperature. "It looks like you've got yourself a cold. Drink plenty of fluids, like orange juice, and get some rest," she said.

"Here is a treat for being such a wonderful patient."

Dr. Sinha reached into her pocket and pulled out a sticker that read "Superstar Patient!"

George felt a little better already. He didn't need to be worried about seeing the doctor after all!

As soon as they got home, George climbed back under the blanket and the man tucked him in.

He gave George a big bowl of chicken soup and they watched a movie until George fell asleep.

The next day, George was still a little sniffly, but he was feeling better.

It was a good thing, because today George was having a playdate with his friend Sam.

"I'm sorry, George," said the man, "but I think we should postpone your playdate. I know you're feeling better, but you should still take it easy today. Besides, you wouldn't want Sam to catch your cold, would you?"

George was disappointed. He had been looking forward to seeing Sam.

Reluctantly, he snuggled onto the couch.

"I need to go to the store, but I'll be right back," said his friend. "Remember, Dr. Sinha said you need plenty of rest and fluids."

That gave George an idea. If rest and fluids made him feel a little better today, maybe a big dose of both would cure him of his cold by tomorrow. Then he could play with his friend!

George grabbed every blanket and pillow he could find and added them to the couch.

The pile grew higher and higher. Soon he had a mountain of blankets and pillows.

He climbed to the top for a rest, but—oh no! The pile came tumbling down!

Maybe it was time for some orange juice. George went to the kitchen and found the carton of juice in the refrigerator. He got a glass from the cupboard, but there wasn't enough orange juice to fill it.

He wondered: Where could he get more orange juice? He looked in the refrigerator again and saw a big bag of oranges.

George knew orange juice came from oranges. If he squeezed all of the oranges in the bag, then he'd have plenty of juice!

He squeezed one into his glass, but only a little juice came out. He tried squeezing two at the same time, but he still didn't get much juice.

George had an idea. If he squeezed all the oranges at the same time, maybe he could fill his whole glass!

He squished the bag first with his hands and then with his feet. The bag was filling with juice.

Maybe if he jumped on it, even more juice would come out!

George jumped up and down and up and down on the bag.
He was having so much fun that he didn't notice the man with
the yellow hat standing in the doorway.

"George, what's going on here?
Look at this mess," said the man.

The kitchen had puddles of juice everywhere.
And there were blankets and pillows all over the living room floor.

George pointed to the orange juice and then the blankets. "Oh, were you trying to follow Dr. Sinha's orders?" asked his friend. George nodded. The man smiled.

"Well, this might make it easier." He pulled a new carton of orange juice out of his grocery bag.

He filled George's glass with juice. Then they cleaned up the kitchen and put away the extra blankets and pillows.

George settled down on the couch and the man read him a story while he drank his juice.

The next day, George was finally able to play with his friend Sam.

George was finished with catching colds. He was ready to play catch for real!